THE RED BADGE
OF COURAGE

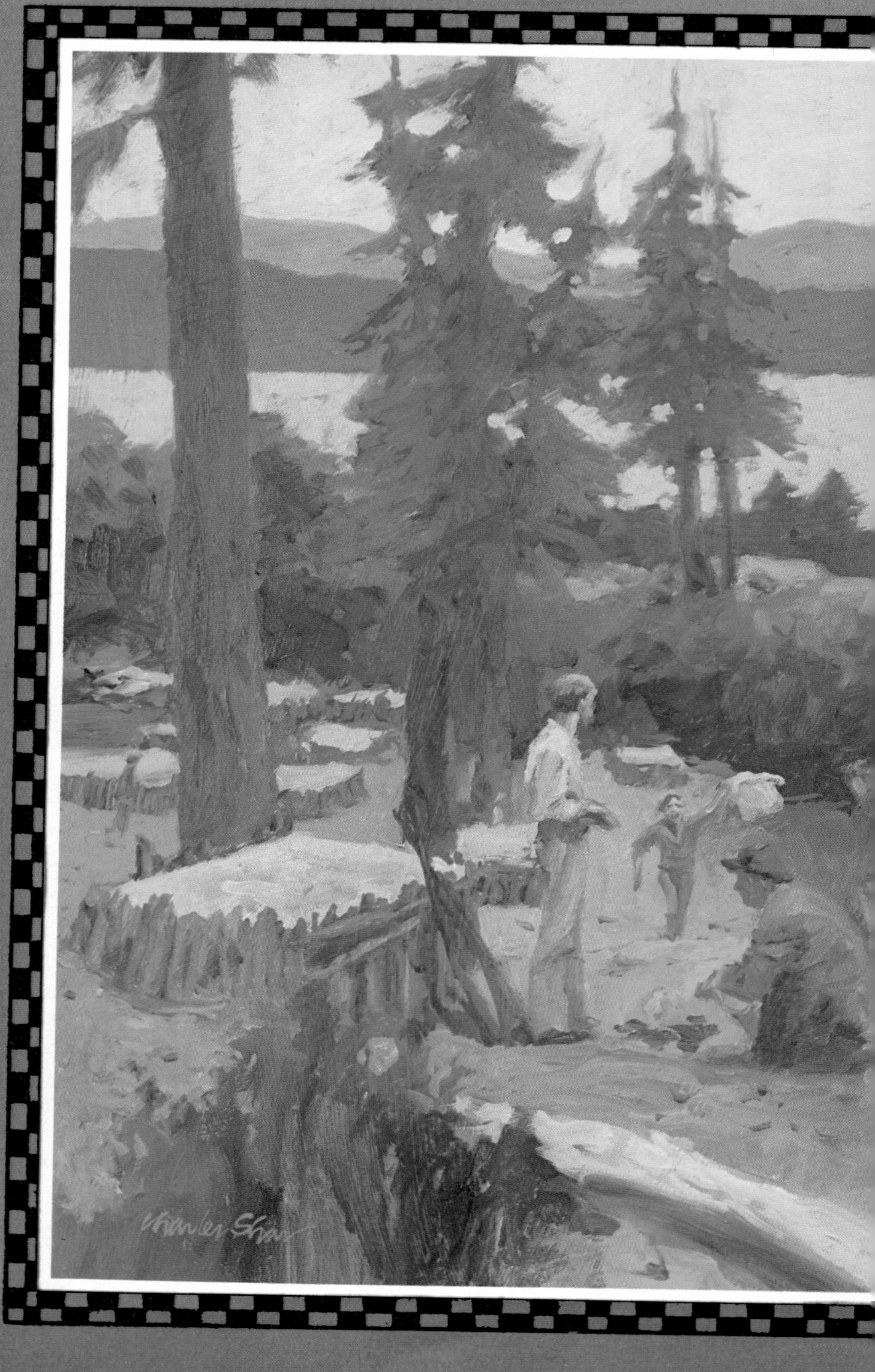

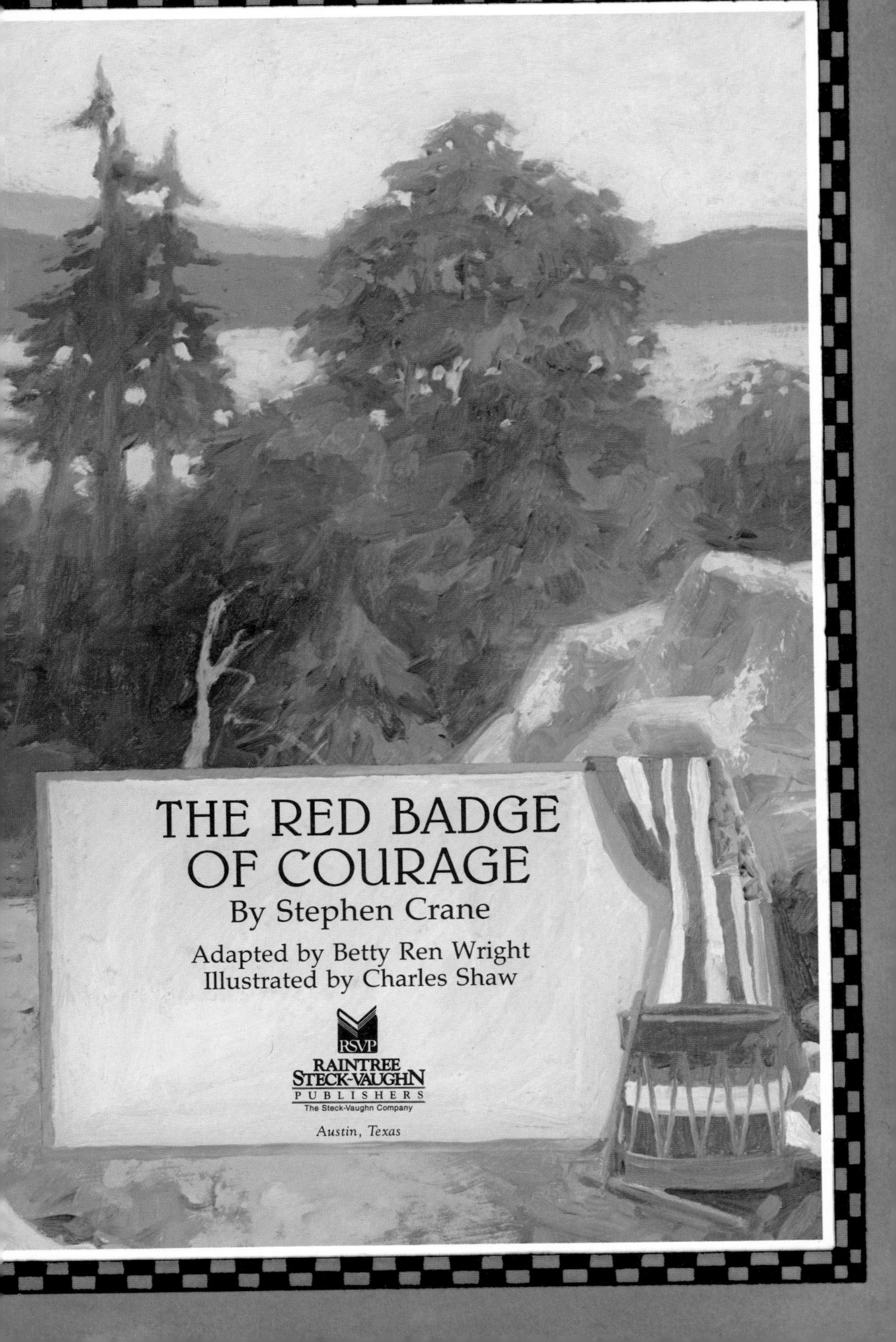

THE RED BADGE OF COURAGE

By Stephen Crane

Adapted by Betty Ren Wright
Illustrated by Charles Shaw

RSVP
RAINTREE
STECK-VAUGHN
PUBLISHERS
The Steck-Vaughn Company

Austin, Texas

Chapter 1
Context clues
Chapter 2
Character Analysis
Chapter 3
Inferencing
Chapter 4
Multi Meaning

l
n
a

Ju
18
Ste
Ser
PZ

ISBN

ISBN _____ 2 softcover binding

18 19   99

CONTENTS

Chapter 5
Context Clues
Chapter 6
Multi Meaning
Chapter 7
Drawing Conclusio

CHAPTER ONE

The cold passed from the earth, and the fog lifted. An army rested on the hills. As the view changed from brown to green, the men woke up. They looked at the river, beyond which one could see enemy campfires.

A certain tall soldier went to wash a shirt. He came flying back with a tale he had heard from a friend.

"We're goin' to move tomorrow, sure," he said to a group in the company street. "We're goin' up the river, cut across, and come around behind 'em."

"It's a lie, a thunderin' lie!" said one private loudly. "I don't believe the army's ever goin' to move. I've got ready to move eight times in the last two weeks, and we ain't moved yet."

The tall soldier felt called upon to prove the truth of his story. He and the loud one came near to fighting over it.

A young private listened eagerly to the words of the tall soldier. After a while he went to his hut and crawled through the hole that served as a door. He wished to be alone with some new thoughts that had come to him.

So at last they were going to fight. Tomorrow, perhaps, he would be in a battle. He could hardly believe that he was to be part of one of those great affairs of the earth.

He had dreamed of battles all his life. But in truth he believed that the time of wars had past. He had looked upon the war in his own country with distrust. It must be some sort of a play affair, he thought.

Still, he had wanted to enlist. One night, as he lay in

bed, he heard the church bell ringing to announce news of a great battle. The next morning he had gone to town and had joined a company that was forming there. When he returned in his soldier's clothes, he had seen tears on his mother's cheeks.

"You watch out, Henry," she said. "Don't go thinking yeh can lick the whole rebel army, because yeh can't. And don't ever do anything that you wouldn't want me to know about. Jest think as if I was watchin' yeh. If yeh do that, I guess yeh will come out about right."

On the way to Washington, the youth's spirit had soared. At each station he was treated as a hero, and he felt himself ready to do mighty deeds. But since he had reached camp he had done little but sit still and try to keep warm. He was brought back to his old ideas that the time of great battles had passed.

Now that he might soon be fighting, he had a serious problem. He had to make himself believe he would not run from a battle. Fear grew in his mind.

"Good Lord, what's the matter with me?" he said aloud.

After a time the tall soldier and the loud private came into the hut. They were still arguing.

"Jim!" The youth spoke to the tall soldier. "How do you think the regiment will do in a fight? Think any of the boys will run?"

"Oh, maybe a few of 'em will," said the other. "You can't bet on nothing. I guess they'll fight better than some, worse than others. I think most of 'em will fight hard, once they get shootin'."

"Do you ever think you might run, Jim?" the youth went on. He laughed as if he were aiming a joke. The loud soldier giggled.

"Well," said the tall private, "I think if a whole lot of the boys started to run, I'd run, too. But if everybody was standing and fighting, why, I'd stand and fight. I'll bet on it!"

"Huh!" said the loud one.

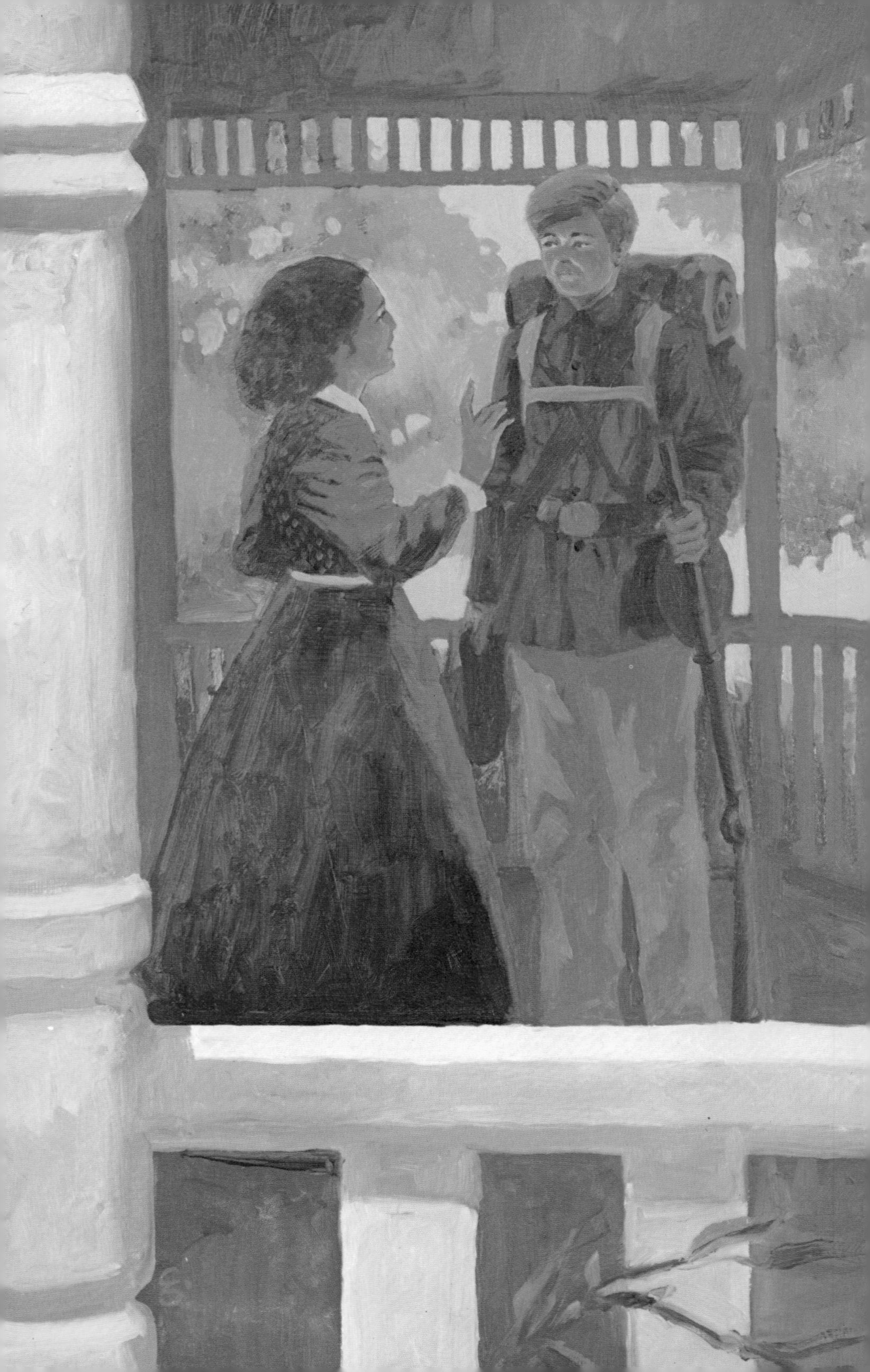

The youth was grateful for the tall soldier's words. He had feared that he was the only one who wasn't sure of what he might do. He felt a little better.

The next morning the youth learned that his tall friend's story had been wrong. There was much teasing from those who had believed it and some sneering from those who hadn't. The tall one fought with one man and beat him.

The youth still worried about what he would do in battle. At last he decided there was no way to be sure. He must see blood and danger before he would know whether he was brave. But meanwhile, he watched his comrades carefully. The tall man's calm manner was helpful, because the youth had known him from childhood. He didn't think that his friend could do anything he himself could not do. Still, the youth would have liked to find someone else who was not so calm. It would have helped to talk about his fears.

He tried to start some talk about what might happen under fire, but his efforts failed. Sometimes he thought all his fellow soldiers must be heroes. Other times he was sure they were as fearful as he was. He wished the generals would not move so slowly, for he wanted an answer to his questions.

At last, early one morning, he found himself in the ranks of his regiment, ready to march. The men swung off into the darkness. From the road came creakings and grumblings as some guns were dragged away.

The youth marched and thought about his problem. He felt apart from his comrades and was saddened by their merry speeches. When one man tried to steal a horse from a farm as they passed, the soldiers cheered the girl who drove him away.

"Hit him with a stick!" they shouted. But the youth took no part.

At night he went early to his tent and wished himself back home.

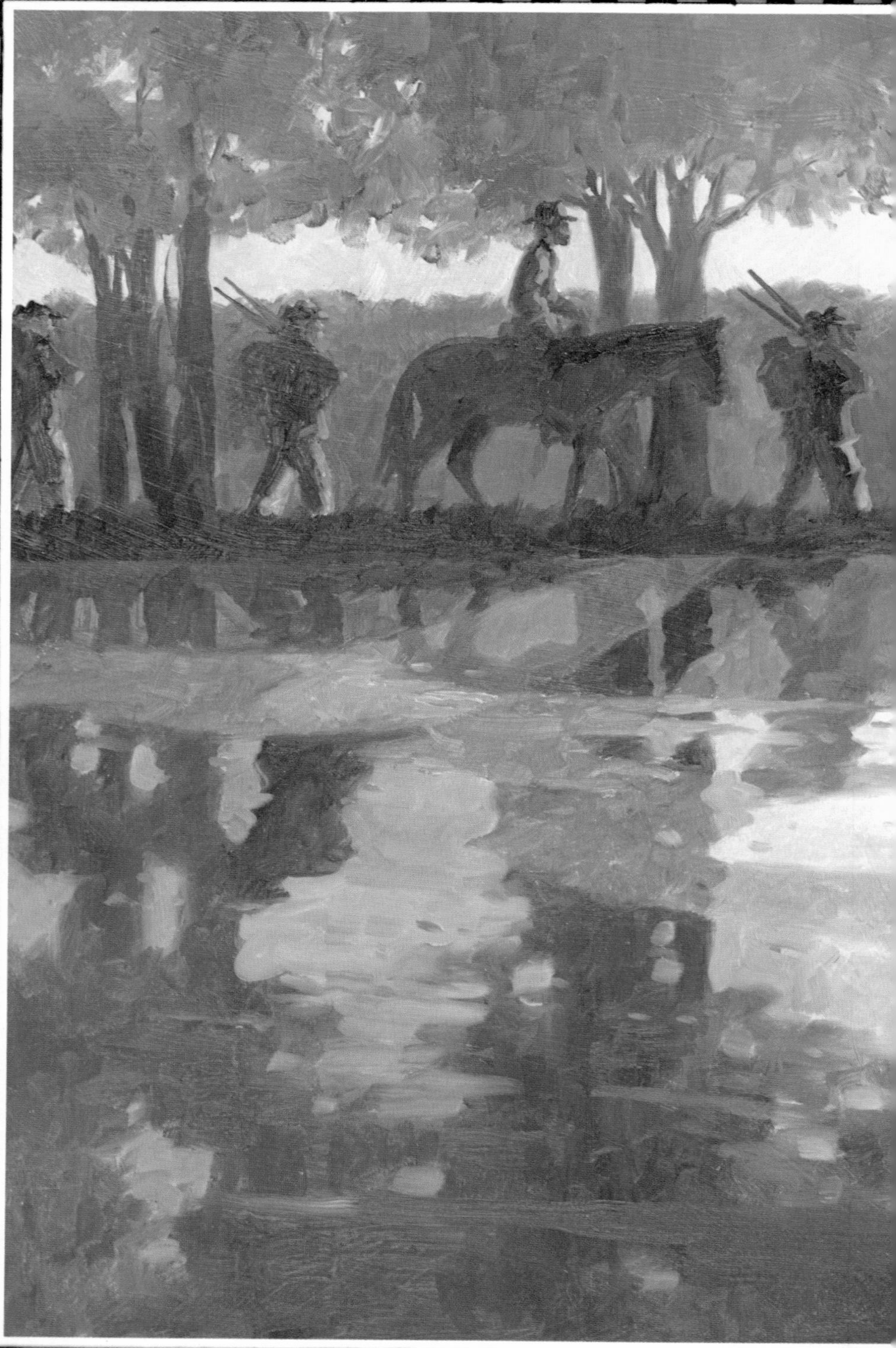

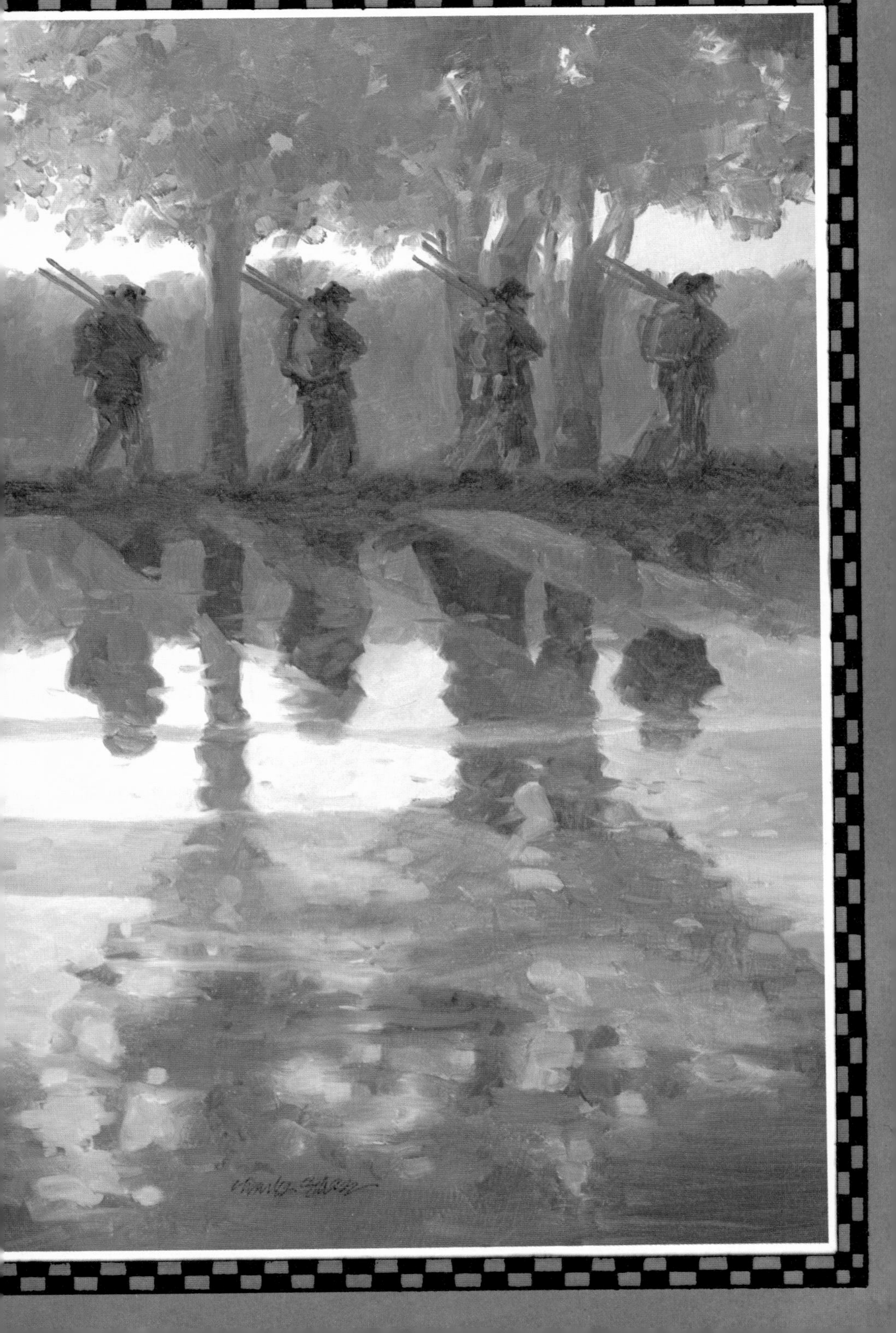

As he lay there he heard a sound and found Wilson, the loud soldier, beside him.

"You're gettin' blue, my boy, " Wilson said. "What's wrong?"

"Oh, nothing," said the youth.

The loud soldier began to talk excitedly about the battle ahead.

"How do you know you won't run when the time comes?" asked the youth.

"Run?" said the loud one. "Of course not!"

"Oh, shucks!" said the youth bitterly. "You ain't the bravest man in the world, are you?"

"I didn't say I was!" exclaimed the loud soldier. "But I'm goin' to do my share of fighting, I am!" He glared at the youth for a moment, then strode away.

The youth felt worse than ever. He stared at the light of the fire on the wall of his tent until he fell asleep.

CHAPTER TWO

When another night came, the marchers filed across two bridges. After the crossing, the youth expected they might be attacked, but they were not. The next day they marched on.

The men had begun to count the miles. "Sore feet and short rations," grumbled the loud soldier. Some of them dropped their knapsacks, keeping only what they were sure they would need.

Presently they made camp, and a painful waiting began once more. Then one morning the youth was kicked in the leg by the tall soldier. Before he was entirely awake he found himself running down a road with his comrades.

"What's all this about?" men whispered. "What are we runnin' for?"

When the sun rose, the youth saw regiments all around them, and he knew the time had come to fight. He was about to find out if he was brave.

As they climbed a hill, guns began to boom on the other side. The youth expected to see a battle when he reached the top. What he saw instead were little fields squeezed by a forest. Here and there troops were running about and firing. A flag fluttered.

The youth no longer wanted to enter the battle. If he had seen in front of him the kind of battle he expected, he might have felt differently. But the view frightened him. The woods were full of hidden enemies. They were marching into a trap!

He wanted to warn his comrades, but they did not appear worried. They would laugh at his warning.

"Come, young man!" shouted the lieutenant. "No hanging back!"

The youth hated him.

The marchers paused, and the men began to build little hills in front of them. In a short time, however, they were ordered to move. This moving went on all morning, with the men building little hiding places at each stop.

The youth began to think it would be better to get killed at once and end his troubles. He would die and go to a place far from such men as the lieutenant.

Then the brigade ahead of them went into action with a roar.

The loud soldier came up to him. "This is my first and last battle, old boy," he said. "I want you to take these things — to — my — folks." He handed the youth a little pack of letters.

"Why, what —" began the youth. But the other gave him a glance as if from the tomb, raised a limp hand, and turned away.

The brigade halted near a grove. The men crouched among the trees and tried to look beyond the smoke. They could see running men, and they tried to guess what was happening.

The din grew louder. A shell screamed over their heads and landed in the grove. Bullets began to whistle among the branches and nip at the trees.

The battle flag they had been watching suddenly sank down as if dying. Wild yells came from behind the walls of smoke, and men were seen to gallop back like wild horses.

The older regiments on the right and left of the 304th began to jeer, but the youth and his comrades were filled with horror.

"Saunders got crushed!" whispered a man at the youth's side.

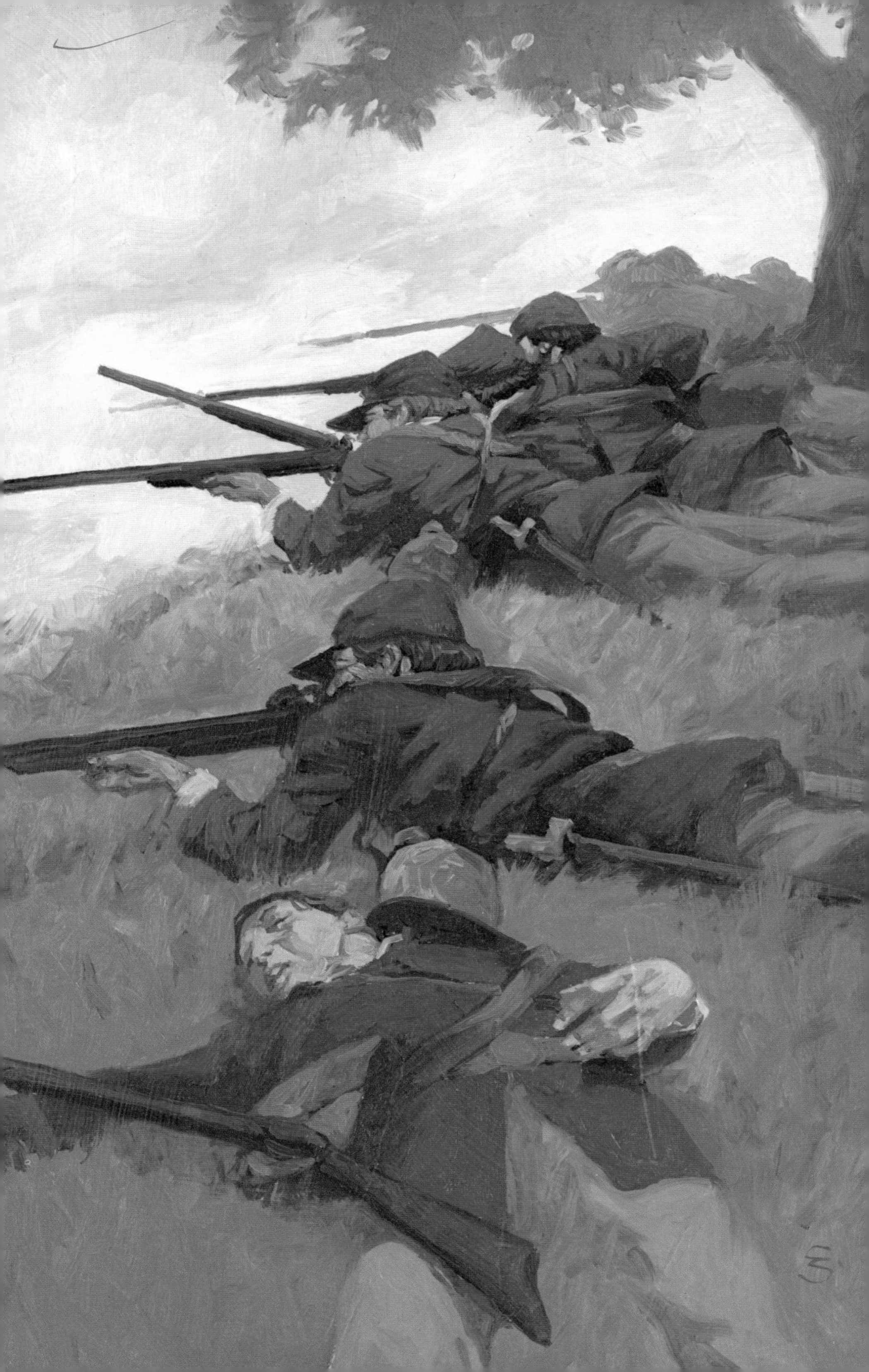

They watched the beaten men run past them. Officers shouted and struck about them, but they could not stop the retreat. When the youth looked at the running men's faces, he felt that he would have joined them if he had been able to make his legs move.

He had one little thought in the midst of it all. He had not yet seen the battle-monster that had caused the other troops to flee. He would get a view of it, and then, he thought, he might very likely run better than the best of them.

There were moments of waiting. The youth thought of a street at home before a circus parade began. He remembered how he had waited then.

Someone cried, "Here they come!" Gunlocks clicked.

A swarm of men came running across the fields with shrill yells. A flag, tilted forward, sped near the front.

The captain of the company paced behind them. "Hold your fire, boys — don't shoot till I tell you — wait till they get close —"

The youth fired a first wild shot. He began working his weapon without pause. He became not a man but a member of an army. His comrades were all about him, and he did not think about running. He loaded his rifle and fired, again and again.

Soon he began to sweat. A burning roar filled his ears. Following this came a red rage. The smoke and din filled him with anger. All around him, his comrades were cheering, snarling, or praying. They loaded their rifles and fired into the smoke without aiming. Behind them, the officers howled their orders. Here and there men dropped like bundles.

The captain of the youth's company had been killed almost at once. A comrade close by grunted suddenly as if he had been struck by a club, and another had his knee splintered by a ball. He dropped his rifle and gripped a tree with both arms. There he remained, crying for help.

At last a yell went along the line. The firing slowed and the smoke drifted away. The charge had been thrown back. The youth grasped his canteen and took a long swallow.

"Well, we've held 'em back!" the men said.

The youth looked around him. Nearby a few forms lay still. Guns roared from the rear of the grove. A small parade of wounded men moved drearily toward the rear. To the right and left were the dark lines of other troops still fighting. The youth saw the flags among them and was thrilled at the sight. They were like beautiful birds flying in a storm.

Then he looked up and felt a flash of astonishment at the blue sky and the gleaming sun. It was surprising that Nature had gone on with her golden work in the midst of so much devilment.

CHAPTER THREE

So it was all over at last! The great test had been passed. The youth was very pleased with what he had done. He thought about what had happened and decided that the man who had fought thus was very brave.

He turned to his comrades with good will. "Gee, ain't it hot?" he said to one who was polishing his wet face with his sleeve. Then he helped another soldier bind up a wound of the leg.

Suddenly cries of amazement broke out along the ranks. "Here they come again! Here they come again!"

The youth turned quick eyes to the field. He saw forms swelling out of a distant wood. The shells came swirling in once more.

The youth stared. Surely this thing was not about to happen. He waited for the enemy to stop and admit it had made a mistake. But firing began along the line and spread on both sides. The smoke of battle rolled over them all.

The youth's neck quivered with weakness. His arms felt numb. His hands seemed too large, and he could hardly move his knees. He slowly lifted his rifle and shot, then shut his eyes and waited as if to be gobbled up by a dragon.

Near him a man stopped shooting and ran away. Another followed. Others began to scamper through the smoke. The youth looked around him and saw the few running forms. He yelled in fright and followed them toward the rear in great leaps.

He ran like a blind man. His rifle and cap were gone. Two or three times he fell. He thought that all the regiment was fleeing.

Shells hurtled over his head with wild screams. Once one landed in front of him and he fell to earth, then leaped up and ran again.

As he ran he saw gunners firing their cannons. Why didn't they run, too? He saw a brigade moving forward and scrambled to a small hill to watch. What manner of men were they, anyhow? Perhaps they didn't understand what was happening — the fools.

Then he saw a general sitting on his horse and taking reports from his staff. As he watched, he saw the general bounce excitedly in his saddle.

"They've held 'em!" he exclaimed. "They've held 'em!" He beamed upon the earth like a sun.

The youth felt as if he had been caught in a crime. They had won after all! The line had remained, and they had won. He could hear cheering.

He turned away, amazed and angry. He had run, he told himself, because he was a little piece of the army, and it was the duty of every little piece to save itself. Later the officers could fit the little pieces together again.

He thought bitterly of his comrades who had held the line. They had shown poor sense in staying, he told himself. But he could almost hear the jeers that would greet him when he returned to camp. He shambled along with bowed head. He looked like a criminal who thinks both his guilt and his punishment are great.

He went into a thick woods. After a time the sounds of battle grew faint. The quiet forest calmed him. At length he reached a place where tall trees made a chapel. He pushed aside the green branches and entered. Then he stopped, horror-stricken.

He was being looked at by a dead man seated against a tree. The eyes stared. The mouth was open. Ants ran over the face.

19

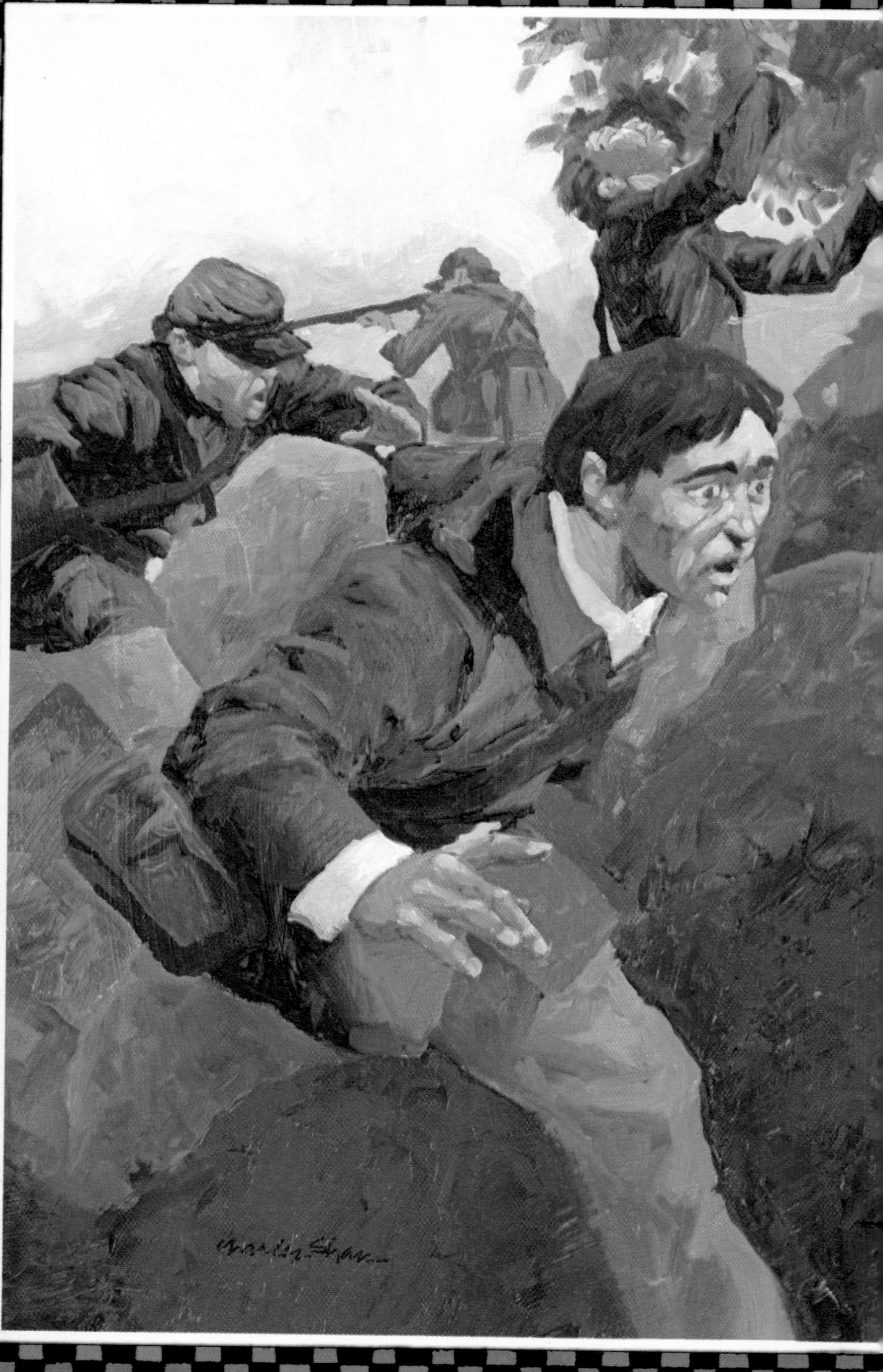

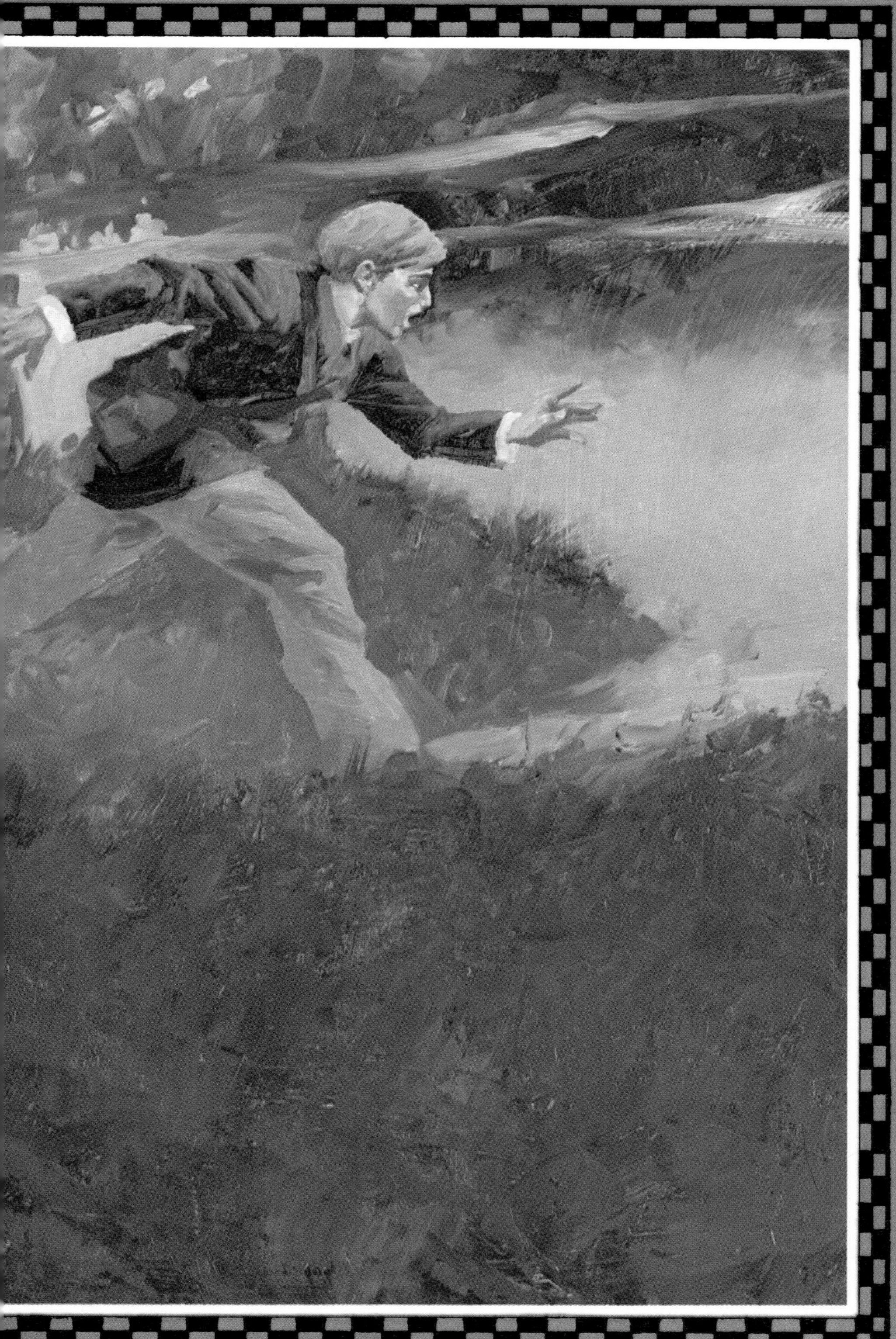

The youth gave a shriek. At first he could not move, but then he backed away, step by step. He did not dare to turn his back for fear the body might spring up and chase him.

At last he was able to run. He sped away, not heeding the underbrush. When he paused, he thought he might hear some strange voice that would come from that dead throat and squawk after him.

The trees around the forest-chapel moved in the soft wind. A sad silence was upon the spot.

A tremendous sound broke upon the stillness. It was as if worlds were being ripped apart. The youth began to run toward the sound, wishing to see what was happening.

He realized as he ran that the fight he had been part of must have been a small one. Listening to this din, he doubted that he had seen a real battle. He went rapidly on, wishing to come to the edge of the forest so that he could peer out.

He climbed a fence and came on a place where dead soldiers lay all about. He hurried on until he reached a road, and here he saw a crowd of wounded moving to the rear. Through the mighty swell of sound, he could hear the groaning of the wounded.

One man had the gray seal of death already upon his face. His lips curled in hard lines, and his hands were bloody from where he had pressed them upon his wound. He seemed to be awaiting the moment when he would fall forward.

The youth joined the crowd and marched with it. A tattered man walked quietly at his side. After a time he moved near the youth and spoke.

"Was a pretty good fight, wasn't it?"

"Yes," the youth said. He walked faster.

The other hobbled after him. He had two wounds, one in the head, the other in the arm.

"Never saw fellows fight so," he said. "This time they showed what they was. They fighters, they be!" He turned to the youth. "Where yeh hit, old boy?" he asked.

The youth felt panic. "Why," he said, "I — I — that is —"

He turned and slid away through the crowd. The tattered man stared after him in astonishment.

The youth fell back until the tattered soldier was not in sight. Then he walked on with the others. The tattered soldier's question had filled him with shame. He wished that he, too, had a wound — a red badge of courage.

The dying soldier he had seen earlier was at his side. Many men spoke to the man, but he did not answer. His lips seemed to be holding back a moan of great despair. He waved the pitying soldiers away.

Something in the gesture made the youth start as if bitten. He yelled in horror.

"Jim! Jim Conklin!"

The tall soldier made a little smile. "Hello, Henry," he said. "Where yeh been? I thought maybe yeh got keeled over."

"Oh, Jim, oh, Jim —" the youth cried.

The tall soldier seemed suddenly overcome by terror. "I'm afraid I'll fall," he whispered. "And them wagons will run over me."

"I'll take care of you, Jim," the youth wept. "I swear I will." He tried to help, but then the tall soldier seemed to forget his fears. He became the grim, walking figure the youth had seen earlier. He would not take help but said, "No — no — let me be."

"Ye'd better take him out of the road," said a soft voice. It was the tattered soldier. "There's a battery comin', and he'll get run over."

The youth grasped his friend's arm. "Jim, come with me."

The tall soldier turned into a field and began to run. The youth and the tattered man followed, in a strange race.

"Jim — Jim — you'll hurt yourself!"

The tall soldier turned upon them. "Leave me be for a minute, can't yeh?"

He turned and lurched on. At last they saw him stop, his

23

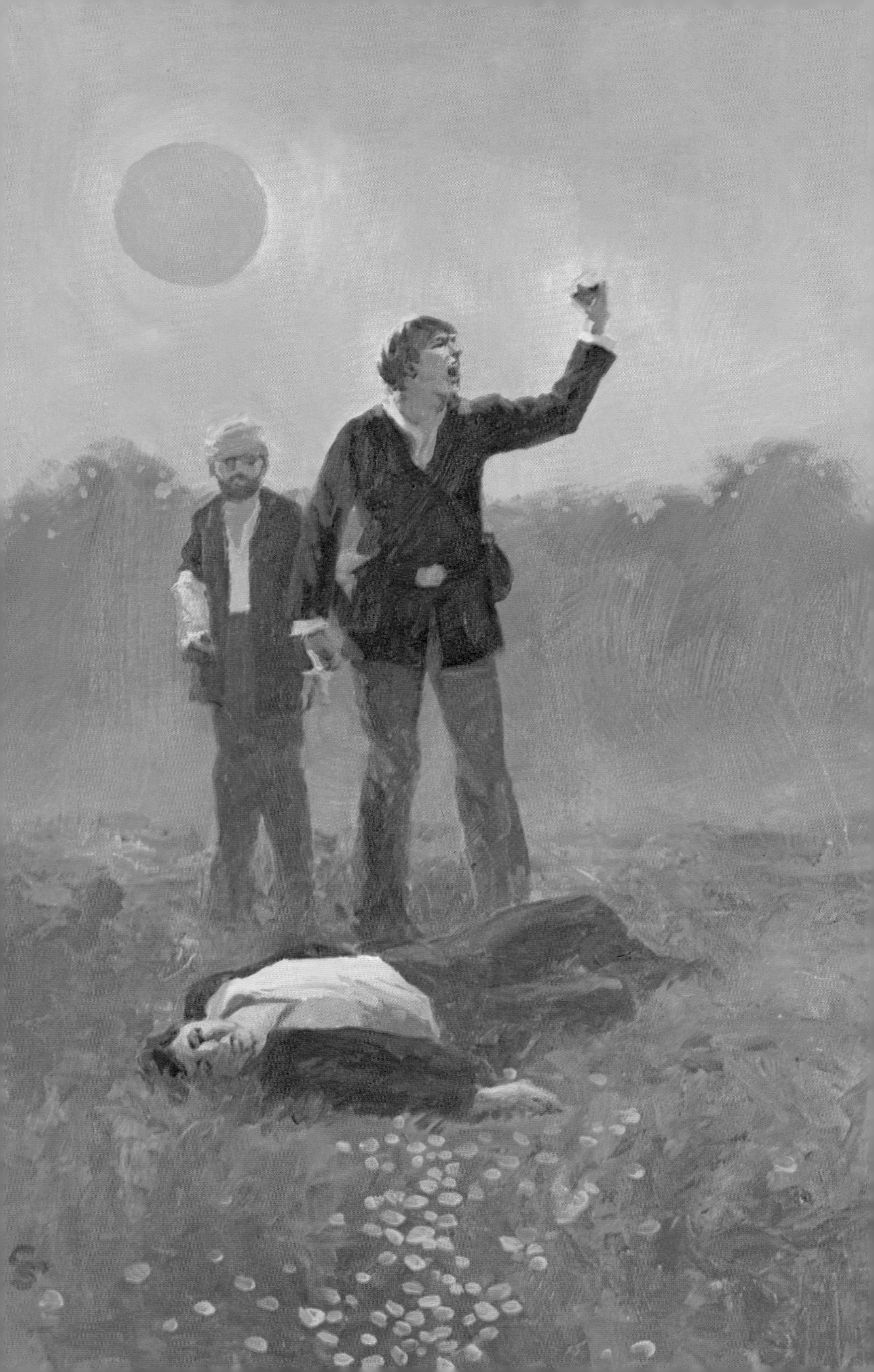

bloody hands at his sides. He seemed to be waiting for something he had come to meet.

"Jim — Jim — Jim —"

"Leave me be." His form stiffened, and his legs moved in a kind of terrible dance. Then his body swung forward like a falling tree.

The youth stared at his friend's dead face. As the flap of the blue jacket fell away, he could see that the side looked as if it had been chewed by wolves.

With sudden rage the youth turned toward the battlefield. He shook his fist as if he were about to deliver a speech.

"Hell —"

The red sun was pasted in the sky like a wafer.

CHAPTER FOUR

"Well, he was regular jim-dandy for nerve, wasn't he?" said the tattered man. "I wonder where he got his strength from."

The youth longed to screech out his grief. He threw himself upon the ground.

"Look here, partner," the tattered man said after a time, "this here thing is all over. He's up and gone, ain't he? Nobody won't bother him. And I must say I ain't enjoying any great health myself."

The youth saw that the tattered soldier's face was turning blue and his legs were unsteady.

"Good Lord," he cried, "you ain't goin' to —"

"Not die," the tattered man said. "But there ain't no use stayin' here. I'm feelin' bad."

They turned their backs on the body of the tall soldier and stole away.

"Yeh look pretty bad yourself," said the tattered man after a while. "Where's your hurt located?"

The youth made an angry motion with his hand. "Oh, don't bother me, " he said. The tattered man's question filled him with shame. "Good-bye," he said suddenly.

The tattered man stared in amazement. "Why — where are yeh goin'?" he asked.

The youth pointed. "Over there." He climbed a fence and started away, trying not to hear his comrade's calls. Once he turned and saw the tattered man wandering helplessly in the field.

The youth wished he was dead. The man's question had been like a knife thrust. He was sure now that his crime would become known. There was no way he could keep it hidden.

The roar of the battle grew louder. As the youth rounded a hill, he saw the road full of wagons, teams, and men. The youth felt the weight of his shame once more. He could never be like these brave infantrymen. They were special beings. He wished he could change lives with one of them and die in battle.

He saw himself flying to the front and performing great deeds. He had no rifle — but rifles lay all around him. And he could fight with another regiment, if he could not find his own. Then he thought of the questions his new comrades might ask, and he knew he could not go through with this plan. He staggered off, sure that he could never become a hero.

Still, he wished to know who was winning the battle. He wanted a victory, of course, but he knew that a defeat might be better for him. It could break up his regiment. Many brave men might desert and run. If there was a defeat, it might prove that he had been right in running when he did.

Then he called himself a villain for wishing such a thing. He must be the most selfish man in the army!

He wished himself dead so he would not have to face the jeers of his comrades. "Where's Henry Fleming?" they would say. "He run, didn't he? Oh, my!" Wherever he went in camp, they would stare and whisper, "There he goes."

He could not make up a story to protect himself against those terrible voices.

The infantry had barely passed when the youth saw dark waves of men sweeping out of the woods. He knew at once that they were retreating. Behind them smoke curled and the voices of cannon were raised.

The youth was filled with horror. He forgot about his own problem. The fight was lost! The dragons of war were coming, and the army was about to be swallowed.

"Why — what's the matter?" he cried. No one answered. He rushed after the retreating mob and clutched one man by the arm.

"Let me go! Let me go!" the man screamed and tried to pull away. The youth was dragged several paces but did not let go.

"Well, then!" bawled the man in rage. He swung his rifle against the youth's head and ran on.

The youth sank to the ground. He tried to get to his feet, but the numbing pain was too much. Deep groans came from his lips. At last he got to his feet and went lurching over the grass.

He struggled on, just as the tall soldier had. He looked for a quiet place where he could fall. Once he put his fingers to his head and found them dabbled with blood. All around him, the retreating army roared by.

"Yeh seem to be in a pretty bad way, boy." A cheery voice spoke, and its owner took his arm. "Well, I'm goin' your way. Guess I can give yeh a lift."

As they walked, the man questioned the youth. "What regiment do yeh belong to? The 304th New York? That's a long way from here, ain't it? Well, I guess we can find it."

The cheery chatter continued, with the man asking questions of guards and patrols along the way. The forest seemed full of men buzzing about in circles, but the cheery soldier seemed to know just where to go. At last he began to chuckle.

"Ah, there yeh are! See that fire?"

The youth nodded.

"Well, there's your regiment. Good-bye, old boy. Good luck to yeh."

A warm hand clasped the youth's fingers, and then the man strode away. As he went, the youth suddenly realized that he had not once seen his comrade's face.

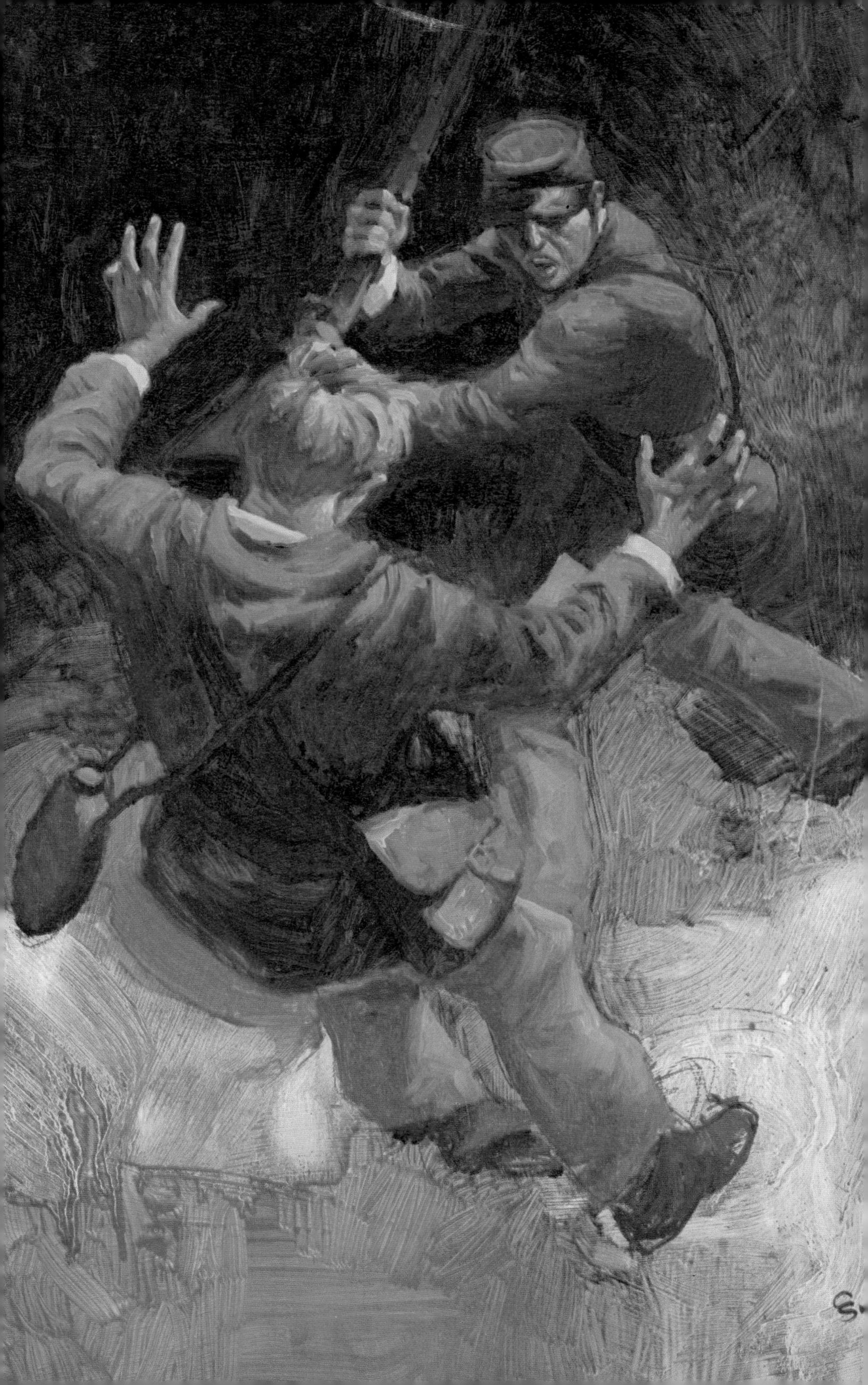

CHAPTER FIVE

The youth went slowly toward the fire. He was sure he was soon to be jeered at, but he was too tired and sore to walk farther.

"Halt! Halt!" A sentry came forward with his rifle up. It was the loud soldier. He peered into the dark.

"Henry! Is it you? I thought yeh was dead sure enough."

The youth staggered. "I've had an awful time, Wilson," he said. "I got separated from the regiment — don't know how. I've been way over on the right. I got shot in the head. I never saw such fightin'."

"What? Got shot? Poor ol' boy!"

Just then the corporal appeared. "Why, hello, Henry, you here? I thought you was dead hours ago. Great Jerusalem, they keep turning up every ten minutes or so!"

"He's got shot in the head," the loud soldier said. The corporal took the youth's arm.

"Put him to sleep in my blanket," the loud soldier said. "I'll come as soon as I'm off duty."

When they reached the fire, the corporal looked at Henry's wound.

"You've been grazed by a ball," he said. "It's raised a queer lump just as if some fellow lammed yeh with a club. You just sit here until Wilson comes to take care of yeh."

He left, and the youth looked at the tired and wounded soldiers around him. Most of them were sleeping. He waited until the loud soldier came.

"We'll fix yeh, Henry," he said. He built up the fire and gave his friend coffee to drink. Then he soaked a handkerchief in water and tied the bandage around the youth's head.

"You're a good one, Henry," he said. "Most men would have been in the hospital long ago. A shot in the head ain't foolin' business. Come on now, lie down and get some sleep."

He spread a rubber blaket on the ground and placed the woolen one about the youth's shoulders.

"Where you goin' to sleep?" the youth asked. "I've got your —"

"Go to sleep," the loud soldier snarled. "Don't be makin' a fool of yourself."

The youth said no more. He gave a long sigh, snuggled down into his blanket, and in a moment was asleep like his comrades.

When the youth awoke, it seemed to him that he had been asleep for a thousand years. His comrades lay sleeping as if dead. He saw his friend adding wood to the fire.

A bugle sounded, and the men began to wake up.

"Well, Henry, how do yeh feel this mornin'?" the loud soldier asked. "Let's see the bandage — I guess it's slipped." He tried to fix the handkerchief in place.

"Go easy!" the youth exploded. "Don't act as if you was nailing down carpet."

"Well, now, come and get some grub," his friend said soothingly. "Then maybe you'll feel better." He hurried to bring some food.

The youth saw that his friend had changed a great deal. He did not brag any more. He was not easily made angry. He was no more a loud young soldier. He seemed strong and sure of himself.

"Jim Conklin's dead," the youth said. "Shot through the side."

His friend started. "Yeh don't say so. Poor Jim."

At this point some soldiers nearby began to argue. The

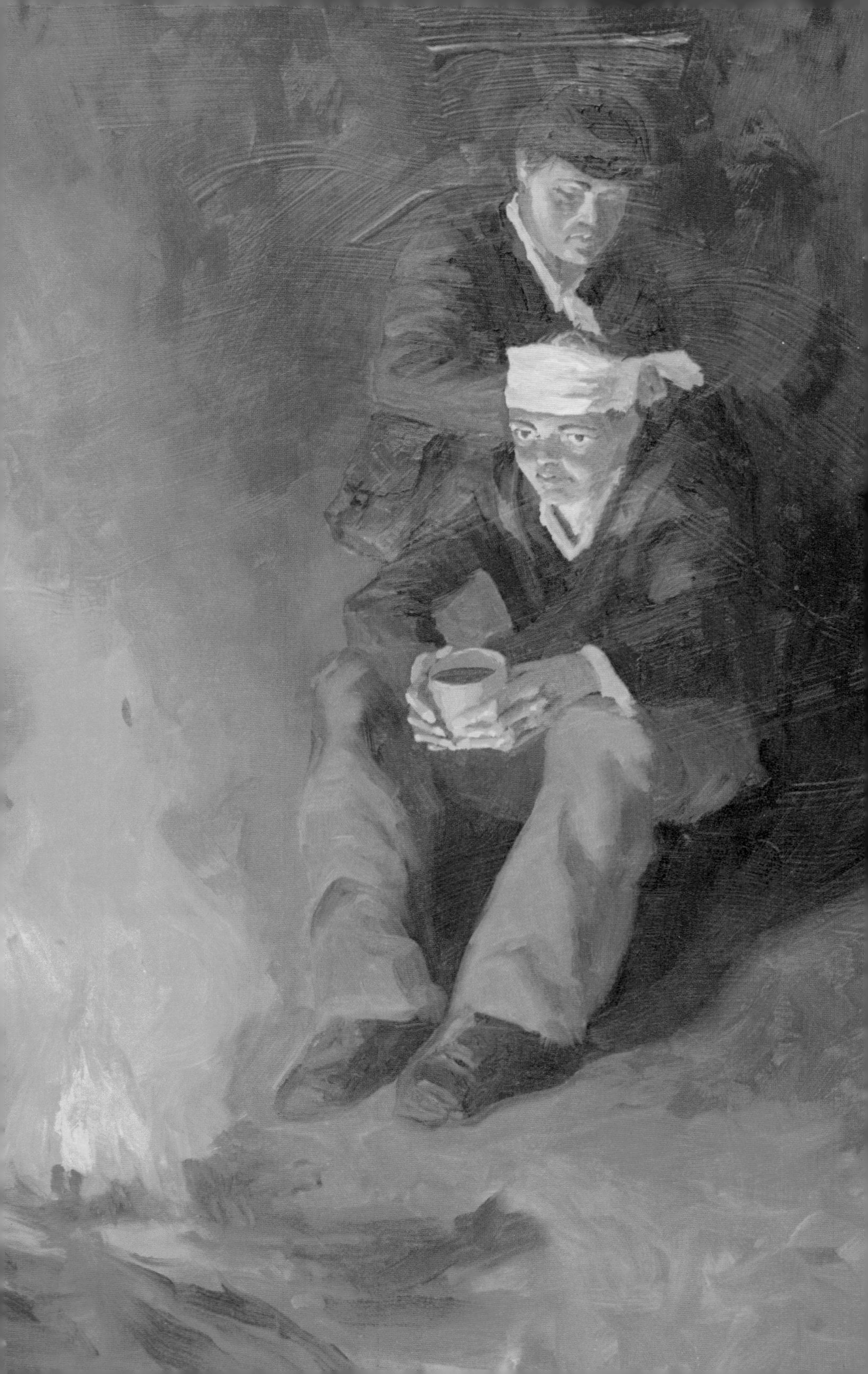

friend arose and went over to them. "We'll be at the rebs in less than an hour," he said. "What's the good fightin' among ourselves."

When he came back, the youth laughed. "You've changed," he said. "You ain't at all like yeh was."

"No," said his friend. "That's true enough." There was a little pause. "The regiment lost over half the men yesterday," he went on. "I thought they was all dead, but they kept comin' back last night until it seems, after all, we didn't lose but a few. They was scattered all around. Just like you."

"So?" said the youth.

While waiting for orders to march on, the youth remembered the pack of letters in his pocket. His friend Wilson had given them to him before their first battle.

He started to call out to Wilson, but then he decided he might keep the letters for a while. Somehow, it made him feel braver to know his friend had been frightened before the battle.

The youth was now much less worried about what had happened. No one knew of his mistake. His panting fear of the past he put out of his sight.

He did not give much thought to the battles that lay ahead. He had learned that some dangers could be avoided. He could leave much to chance. Besides, a faith in himself had begun to grow. He had been out among the dragons of war, and they were not as terrible as he had thought. A stout heart might escape.

He was aroused from his thoughts by his friend's voice.

"Fleming, I guess yeh might as well give me back them letters."

"All right, Wilson," said the youth. He gave the pack to his friend. He saw that Wilson seemed to be suffering great shame. The youth felt his own heart grow more strong. No one had ever seen *him* blush that way.

After that, the youth felt very sure of himself. He

thought about the time when he could tell his mother and his friends about the war. He could hardly wait to tell them how brave he had been among great dangers.

The regiment was waiting to take the place of men who had been in the damp trenches a long time. They lay in the dirt and listened to the sound of battle. There was rifle fire on the left and the roar of cannons on the right.

Just before dawn they were ordered to retreat through the woods.

The youth began to complain about the general who moved them about in this hit-or-miss way. "Don't we fight like the devil?" he demanded. "Don't we do all that men can?"

He was surprised to hear himself say these words. He felt guilty once more.

"Maybe yeh think yeh fought the whole battle yesterday, Fleming," said one of his comrades.

"No, I don't," the youth said quickly. The man said nothing more, but the youth stopped complaining for a moment. He could not bear to be jeered at.

In a clear space the regiment halted and faced the enemy's guns. Once again they waited.

"We're just chased around like rats," the youth grumbled. "It makes me sick!"

"You boys shut up!" the lieutenant shouted. "There's too much chin music and too little fightin' in this war."

They waited, and the battle moved toward them. The soldiers were tired. They had slept little and worked hard. They stood as men tied to stakes.

CHAPTER SIX

The youth beat his foot on the ground and scowled with hate at the smoke drawing close to him. He needed rest. He would like to have talked to his comrades. But the enemy seemed never to get tired.

"If they keep on chasin' us, they'd better watch out," he grumbled. "Can't stand *too* much."

One rifle flashed, and then the whole regiment began to shoot. The youth fought fiercely. Once he fell to the ground, but he was up again without delay. Flames bit him, and the smoke broiled his skin. His rifle grew so hot he could hardly hold it, but he kept on loading and firing.

When the enemy fell back, he moved forward quickly. When he was forced to retreat, he did it slowly. Once he stood all alone, not aware that the others had stopped shooting.

"Yeh fool, don't yeh know enough to quit when there ain't anything to shoot at?"

He turned and saw his comrades staring at him. The smoke was lifting and the enemy was gone.

"By heavens," the lieutenant called to him, "if I had ten thousand wildcats like you, I'd end this war in a week!"

"Do yeh feel all right, Henry?" asked his friend Wilson.

The youth found himself a hero. He saw that this fight had been fine, wild, and, in some ways, easy. He had hardly known what he was doing. It seemed as if he had slept and, awakening, had found himself a knight.

"By thunder," said one of the men, "I bet this army will never see another new regiment like us!"

The ragged line rested for some minutes, but the struggle went on all around them. The ground shook. It was hard to breathe. One man, who was shot through the body, cried out again and again.

The youth's friend offered to go for water, and the youth went with him. They made a quick search but could not find a stream.

As they started back, they looked out over the battle. The air was full of gray smoke and flashes of orange flame. Far off they could see a road filled with retreating soldiers. The shells hooted overhead.

A general and his staff came up. They almost rode over a wounded man. The youth and his friend stood nearby as the officers talked.

"The enemy's formin' for another charge," the general said. "I fear they'll break through unless we try to stop them. Have you troops you can spare?"

One officer, who rode like a cowboy, said, "There's the 304th. They fight like mule drivers. I can spare them best of any."

"Get 'em ready then," said the general. "I don't believe many of your mule drivers will get back."

The youth and his friend hurried back to their comrades. "We're goin' to charge!" they shouted. "We heard 'em talkin'!"

A moment later the officers began to push the men into a tighter mass. They were like shepherds rounding up their sheep.

The youth looked at his friend. They were the only ones who had heard the general's words. "Mule drivers — don't believe many will get back." It was a painful secret, but they did not hold back because of it. They nodded in agreement when a man near them said in a meek voice, "We'll get swallowed."

The youth stared at the land in front of him. It seemed full of unseen horrors. There was a straining among the men, and then the line moved forward.

The youth lunged ahead. His face was hard and his clothes were soiled. With the bloody rag about his head, and his wildly swinging rifle, he looked almost insane.

He did not know he was ahead of the others. Men fell on all sides, and a trail of bodies was left behind.

Presently the pace slowed. "Come on, yeh fools!" the lieutenant bellowed. "Yeh can't stay here!"

The men moved on, more slowly now, stopping every few paces to fire. When they reached an open space they stopped once more.

The lieutenant grasped the youth's arm. "Come on!" he roared. "We've got to go across that lot."

"Cross there?" The youth shook his arm free. "Come on yourself then," he yelled. The two men ran to the regiment's flag, with the youth's friend close behind them.

"Come on!" they shouted. The regiment moved forward again.

Over the field they went — a handful of men into the faces of the enemy. The youth ran like a madman. He ran close to the flag and was filled with love for it. He felt as if it were a saver of lives. A cry went out to it from his mind.

Suddenly he saw that the flag-bearer had fallen to his knees. At once he clutched at the pole. His friend grasped it from the other side. The flag-bearer was dead, but for a grim moment they could not get the flag away from him. At last they wrenched it from his hands, and as they turned away the dead man fell forward. One arm swung high and fell on the friend's shoulder.

When they turned with the flag, they saw that much of the regiment had fallen. What was left was retreating.

The two friends had a small scuffle over the flag.

"Give it to me!"

"No, let me keep it!"

Each was willing to take on the danger of carrying it. Finally the youth pushed his friend away.

The regiment retreated to some trees. They had lost heart. It was as if they had run into walls of stone and knew it was no use to try to go on. The youth went along,

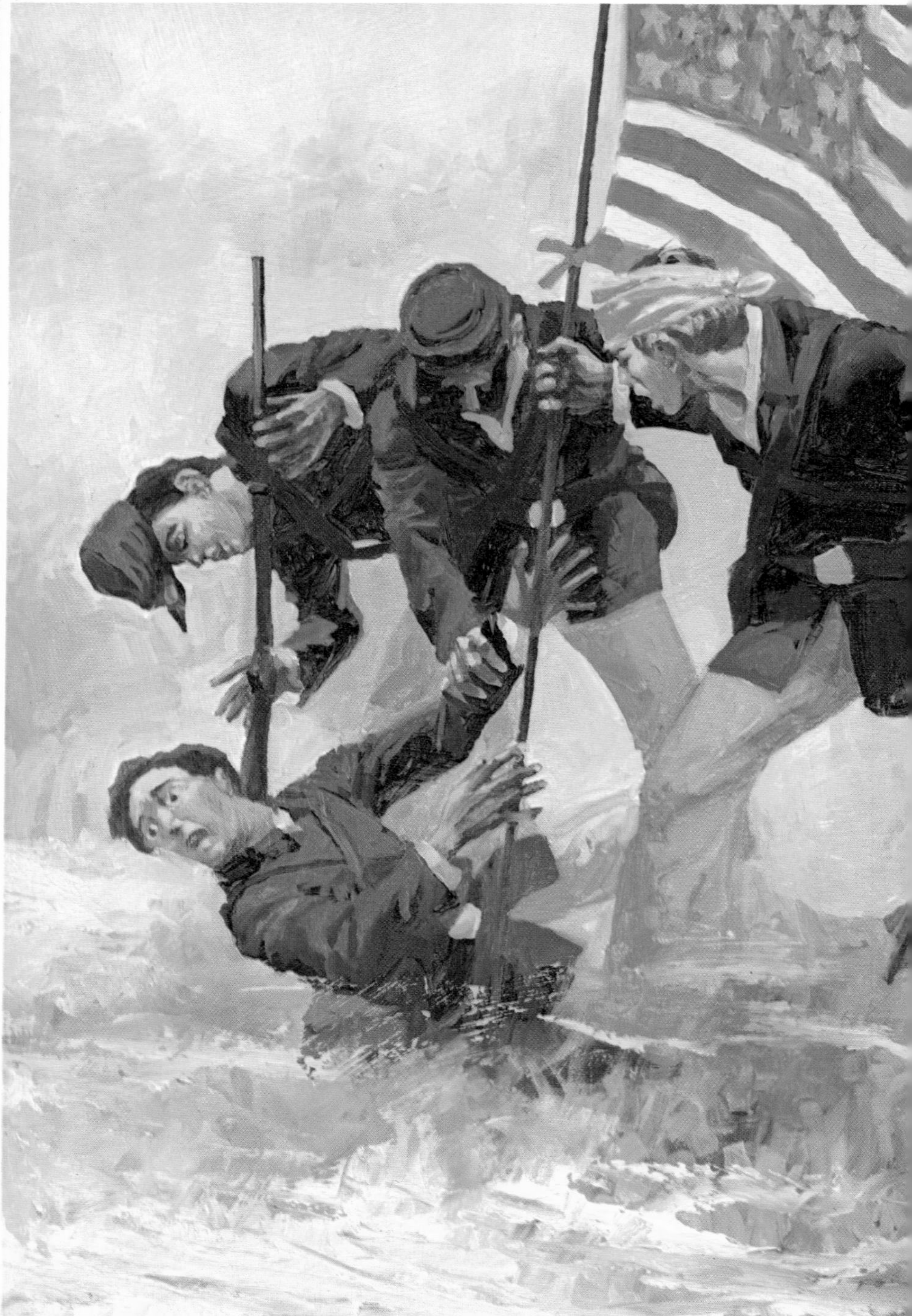

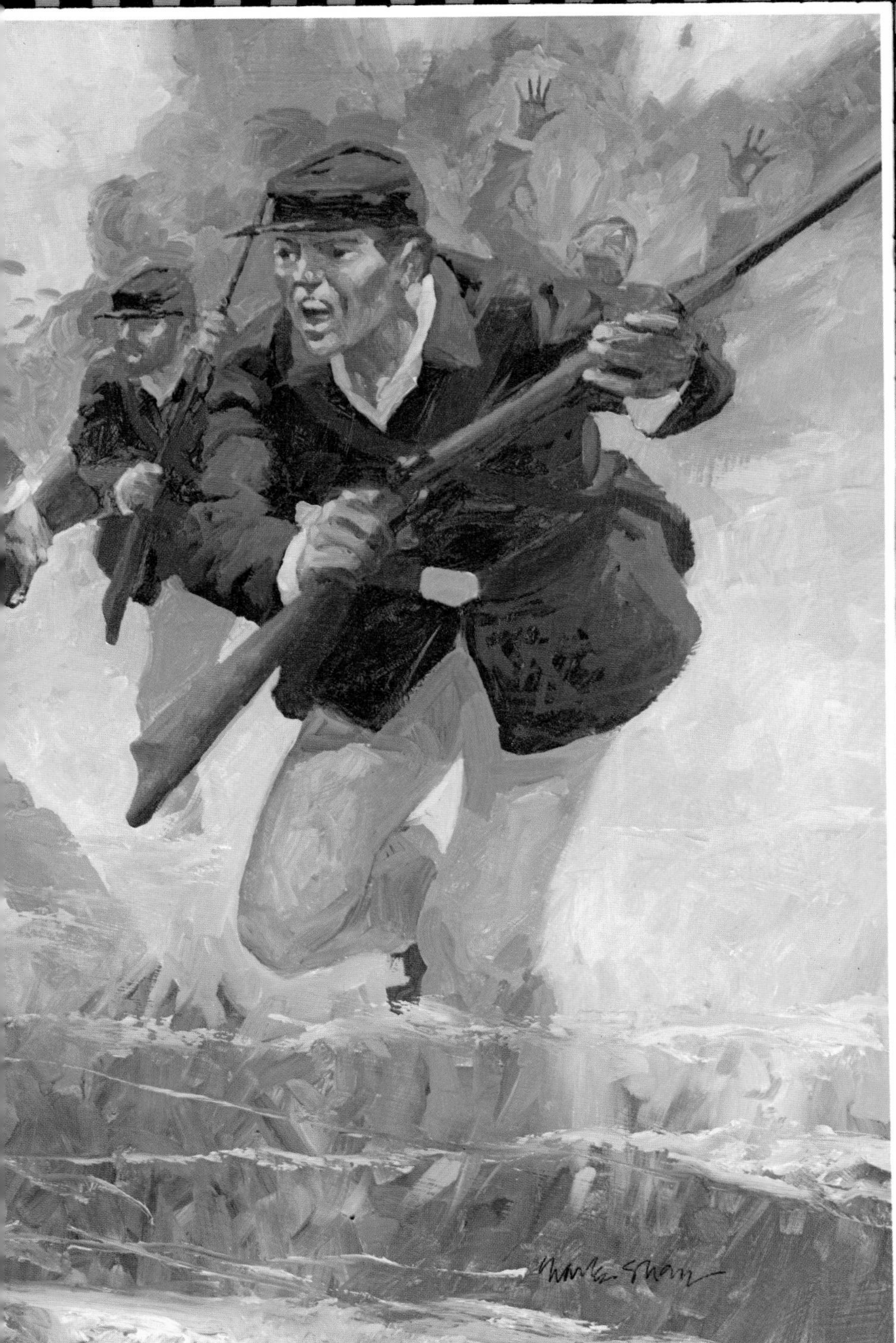

full of shame and rage. He thought about the officer who had called him and his comrades mule drivers. He had wanted to win this battle so the officer would be sorry for what he had said.

He joined the lieutenant in trying to stop the retreat. But the regiment was like a machine run down. Men ran back and forth looking for ways to escape the wall of bullets. The youth walked into their midst and stood with the flag in his hands. He waited, choking in the thick smoke.

"Look! Here they come! Right onto us!" the lieutenant roared.

The youth turned and saw the enemy close by. Their gray uniforms looked fresh. It was clear that they had not known how near they had come to the retreating regiment.

The two bodies of troops exchanged blows like a pair of boxers. The men in gray seemed to draw closer, step by step, and the regiment fired without hope. But then the blows of the enemy began to grow weak. Fewer bullets ripped the air. As the smoke lifted, the men saw that the ground in front of them was empty except for a few dead bodies.

The men in blue sprang to their feet. They danced with joy. A cheer broke from their lips.

It had been a small battle, but it had showed them that they could win after all. They looked about with pride, feeling new trust in their guns and in themselves. They were men.

CHAPTER SEVEN

The firing was behind them. They were free. The little band of men took a deep breath and hurried on toward their own lines. Now that the charge was over, they were strangely frightened. They kept looking over their shoulders, as if they might be shot just when they thought they were safe.

A regiment of older soldiers lay resting under some trees.

"What yeh comin' back for?" they jeered. "Why didn't yeh stay there?"

The youth was hurt by these remarks. He glared at the resting soldiers. But then he turned and looked over the land where they had charged. He was surprised to see what a small distance it had been. It was hard to believe so much had happened in such a little space. Perhaps the old soldiers were right to jeer.

Still, the youth was pleased with what he had done himself.

As they rested, the officer who had called them mule drivers rode up. He looked very angry.

"What a mess you made of things!" he told the colonel of the youth's regiment. "If you had gone a hundred feet farther it would have made a great charge, but as it is — what a lot of mud diggers you have!" He turned his horse and rode away.

"Good thunder!" the men muttered. They thought the officer must have made a huge mistake.

"I wonder what he does want," said the youth's friend. "He must think we went out there and played marbles! I never did see such a man!"

"Well, you and I did good as we could," said the youth.

As they spoke, several men came hurrying up to them.

"O Flem, yeh ought to have heard!" one cried. "The colonel just said to the lieutenant, 'Who was that lad what carried the flag?' 'That's Fleming,' said the lieutenant. 'He and a fellow called Wilson was at the head of the charge all the time.' 'Were they indeed?' says the colonel. 'Well, they deserve to be major generals!'"

"You're lyin'," said the youth and his friend. "He never said it!" But they knew their faces were flushed with pleasure. They looked at each other with joy.

And at once they forgot many things. They were happy, and their hearts were full of liking for the colonel and the lieutenant.

From his resting place, the youth watched the battle around him.

On one side he saw two regiments fighting two other regiments. They fought by themselves, as if they had no part in the larger war. On another side he saw a fresh brigade marching into a wood and out again.

On a slope to the left, a long row of guns blasted the enemy. Some horses, tied to a railing, tried to break away.

When it was his regiment's turn, they moved out fiercely. They aimed through the smoke in front of them. Their eyes were full of hate. The youth, who still carried the flag, watched the battle around him. He saw the enemy come very close. They hid behind a fence and began to fire into the youth's regiment. The men in blue fought fiercely.

The youth made up his mind that he would not move, whatever happened. He might be found dead on the field with the flag in his hands. Then the officer who had called them mule drivers and mud diggers would be sorry for what he had said.

Many of his comrades fell around him. A sergeant was shot through both cheeks, but he went on shouting to the

42

men. The youth looked for his friend. When he saw him, he hardly knew him. He was wild-looking and covered with powder.

Then the youth noticed that the officers' shouts were beginning to fade. The fire of the regiment had become less. The strong voice of the guns was growing weak.

The officers came running along back of the line.

"We must charge them!" they shouted. "We must charge!"

The youth saw that this was true. To stay where they were meant death. They must push the enemy away from the fence.

The other men seemed to agree. Even though they were very tired, they yelled and leaped forward. The youth kept the flag out in front. With his free arm he waved his comrades on.

He felt joy in his own strength. He was ready to die if it must be. He did not think about anything except reaching the fence and driving out the men in gray.

Soon he saw that many of the enemy had begun to retreat. Only one part of the line held firm. The youth's regiment drew close to them. The youth saw the enemy's flag and ran toward it. He wanted to capture it.

Four or five wounded men lay ahead of him. The enemy flag-bearer stood in their midst. He had been badly wounded, but he hugged his flag to him. He looked back as the first men in blue jumped over the fence.

The youth's friend leaped at the enemy flag. He pulled it free just as the flag-bearer fell dead.

The charge was over. The regiment cheered and threw their hats in the air.

At one part of the line, four men had been made prisoners. The blue soldiers walked about them and asked them questions.

After a while the men settled down behind the old fence and rested. There was some long grass. The youth lay in it, after leaning the flag against a rail. His friend came, holding the enemy flag. They sat side by side and told each other how well they had done.

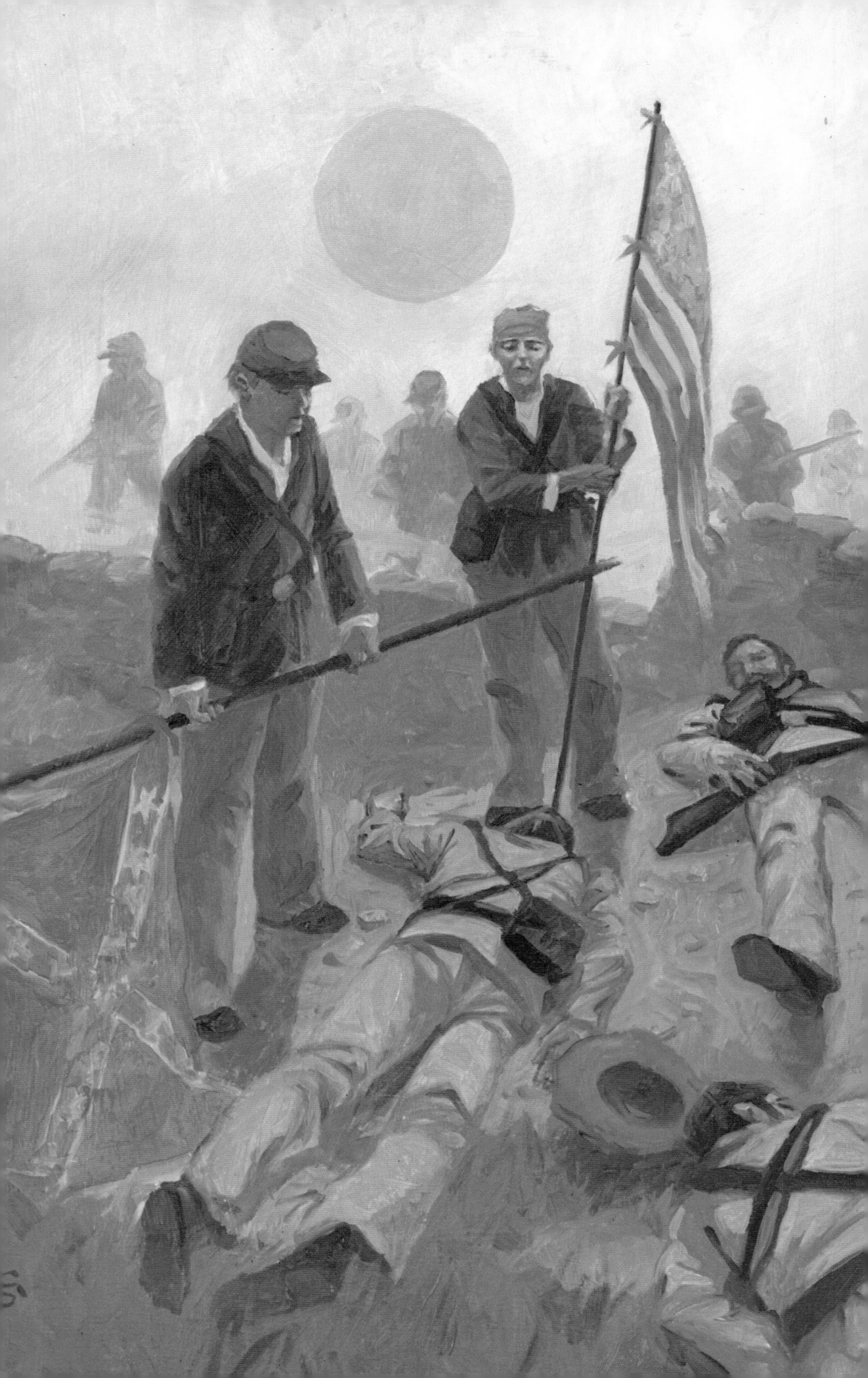

The roarings that had stretched across the forest grew weaker. The youth and his friend looked up and wondered what was to happen next.

"I bet we're goin' to get out of this and go back over the river," the friend said.

They waited, and soon orders arrived to move back. The men rose, groaning and stiff. They moved slowly back over the field they had crossed in a mad scamper. When they met the rest of their brigade, they marched away toward the river.

The youth looked back at the battlefield. "Well, it's over," he said.

It was good to think of the brave things he had done while his comrades were watching. He thought with joy of the time the lieutenant had said, "If I had ten thousand wildcats like you, I could end this war in a week."

But then he remembered how he had run away from his first battle. Once more, he was full of shame. He thought of the tattered soldier who had been with him when the tall soldier died. He remembered that he had left the tattered soldier wounded and alone in a field. He cried out in pain at the memory.

For a time the youth could think of nothing else. He believed the memory of the tattered soldier would stand before him all his life. But at last he forced the thought away. He decided that it was not such a bad thing to make a mistake. It would teach him to do better in the future.

He began to feel that he understood the world better. He knew that he would not run again, no matter what happened. He had been to touch the great death and found that, after all, it was but the great death. He was a man.

It rained. The soldiers muttered against the weather, but the youth smiled. He had rid himself of the red sickness of battle. He turned now to this other world of calm skies, fresh meadows, and cool brooks. A world of peace.

Over the river a golden ray of sun came through the rain clouds.

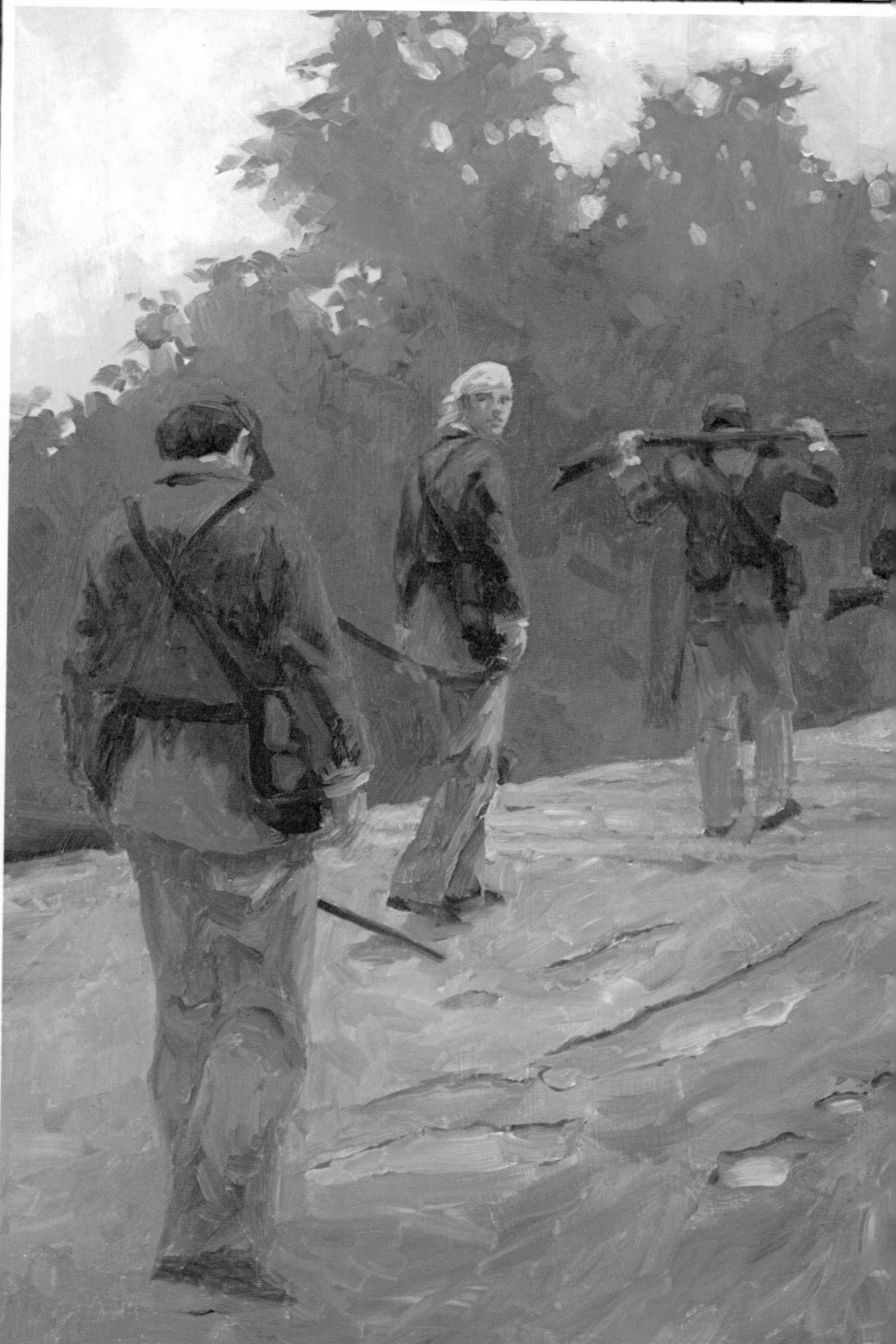

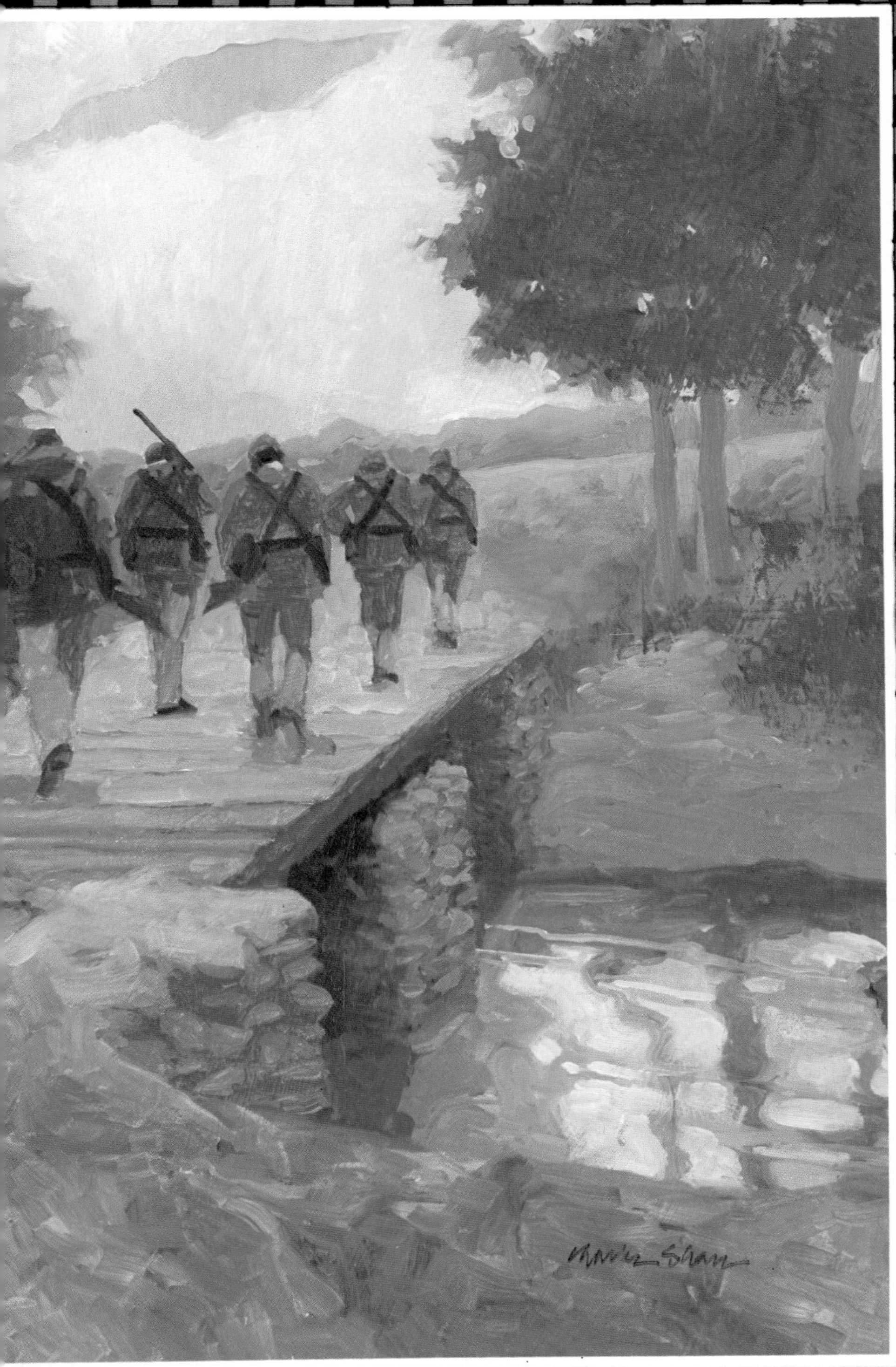

GLOSSARY

battery (bat' ə rē)   a unit of the army made of soldiers and heavy weapons

brigade (brig ād')   a large group of soldiers in an army

company (kəmp' ə nē)   a medium-sized group of soldiers in an army

infantry (in' fən trē)   soldiers that are trained to fight on foot

regiment (rej' ə mənt)   a very large group of soldiers, often made up of many companies

tattered (tat' ərd)   wearing torn or ragged clothes